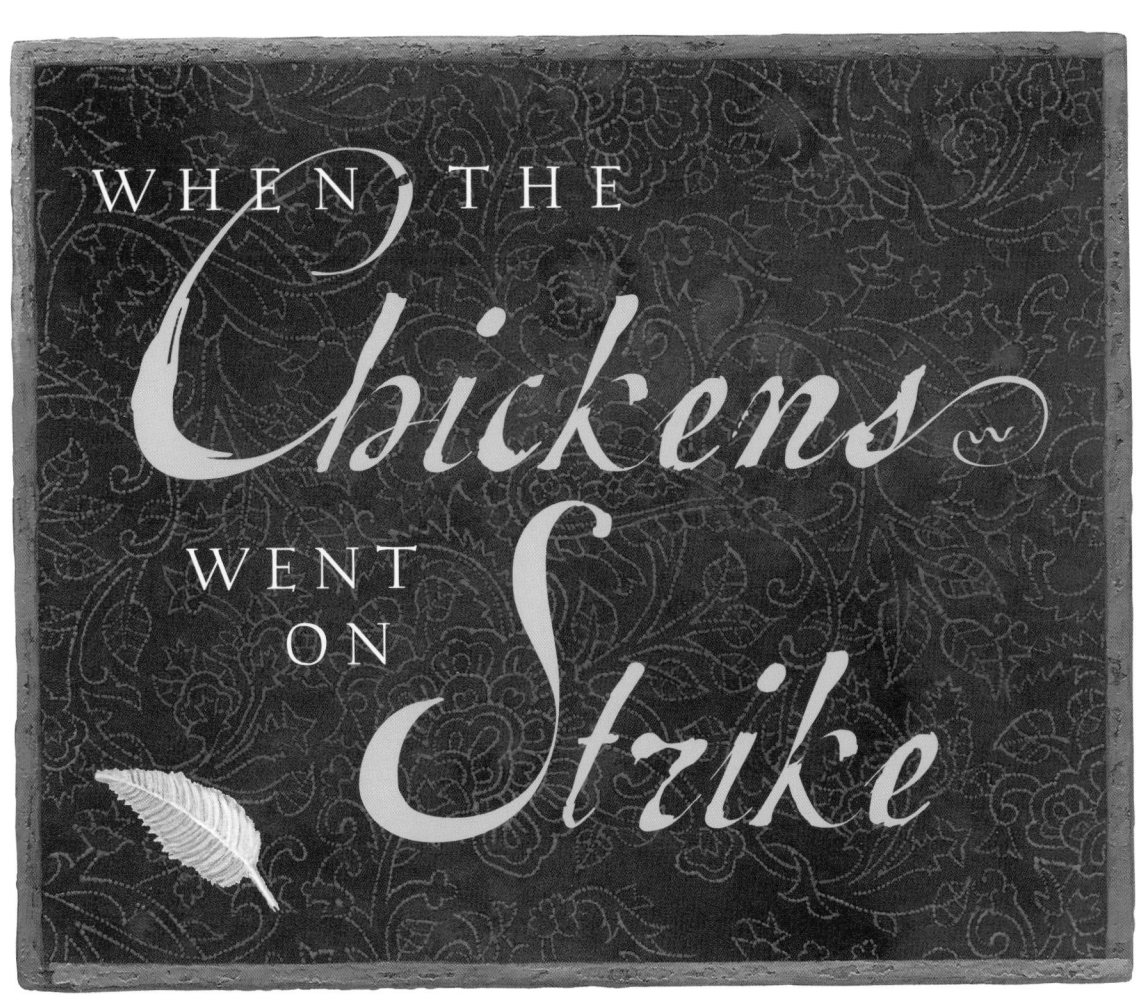

When the
Chickens
WENT
ON
Strike

WHEN

WENT

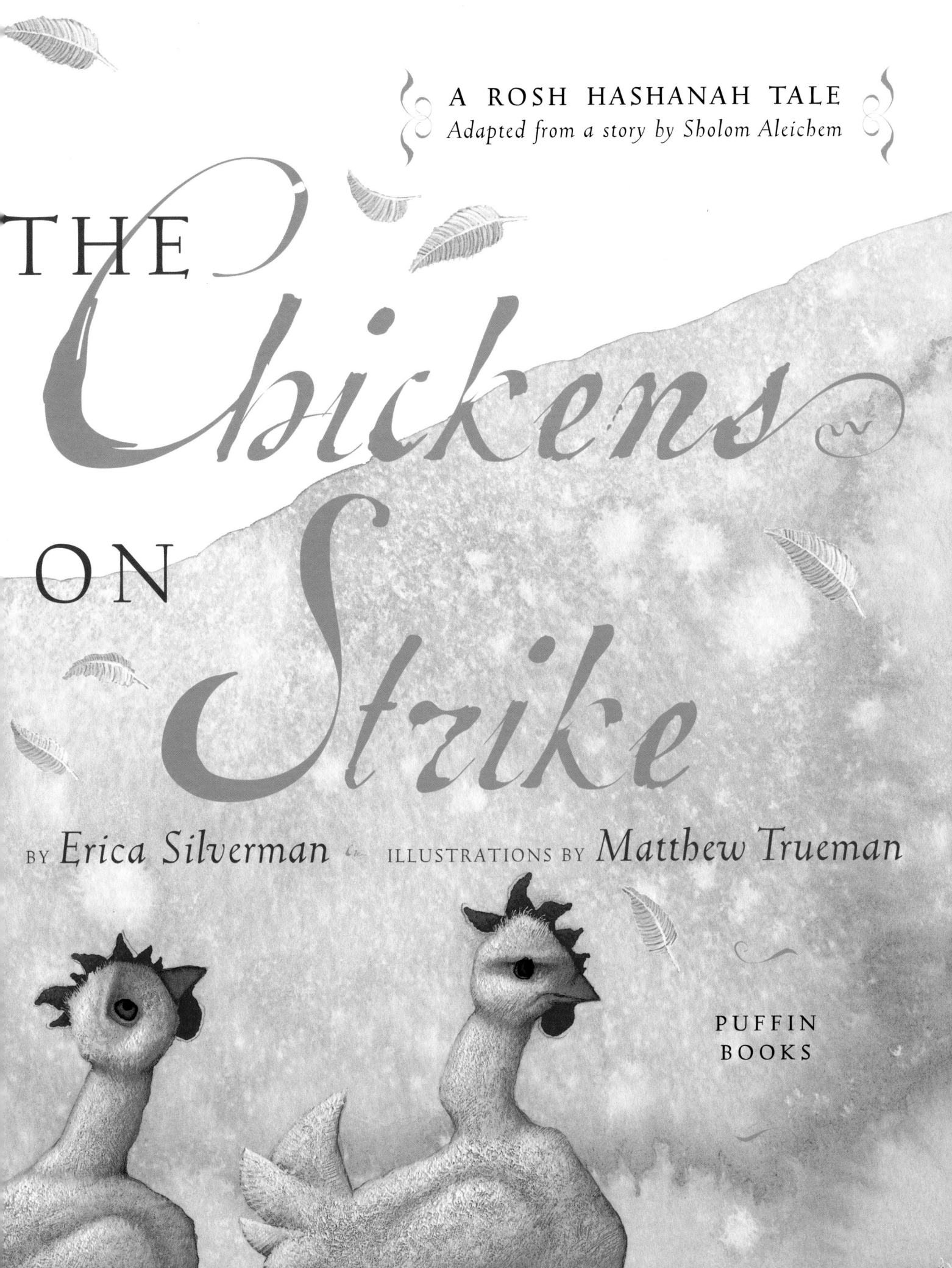

A ROSH HASHANAH TALE
Adapted from a story by Sholom Aleichem

THE Chickens ON Strike

BY Erica Silverman   ILLUSTRATIONS BY Matthew Trueman

PUFFIN
BOOKS

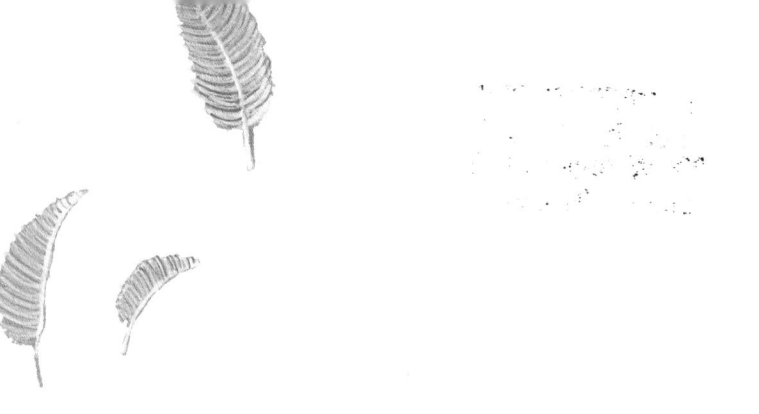

To Sholom Aleichem—E.S.

*For Anna and Michèle,
who made me do it—M.T.*

PUFFIN BOOKS
Published by the Penguin Group
Penguin Young Readers Group, 345 Hudson Street, New York, New York 10014, U.S.A.
Penguin Group (Canada), 10 Alcorn Avenue, Toronto, Ontario, Canada M4V 3B2
(a division of Pearson Penguin Canada Inc.)
Penguin Books Ltd, 80 Strand, London WC2R ORL, England
Penguin Ireland, 25 St Stephen's Green, Dublin 2, Ireland
(a division of Penguin Books Ltd)
Penguin Group (Australia), 250 Camberwell Road, Camberwell, Victoria 3124, Australia
(a division of Pearson Australia Group Pty Ltd)
Penguin Books India Pvt Ltd, 11 Community Centre, Panchsheel Park, New Delhi - 110 017, India
Penguin Group (NZ), Cnr Airborne and Rosedale Roads, Albany, Auckland, New Zealand
(a division of Pearson New Zealand Ltd)
Penguin Books (South Africa) (Pty) Ltd, 24 Sturdee Avenue, Rosebank, Johannesburg 2196, South Africa

Registered Offices: Penguin Books Ltd, 80 Strand, London WC2R ORL, England

First published in the United States of America by Dutton Children's Books,
a division of Penguin Putnam Books for Young Readers, 2003
Published by Puffin Books, a division of Penguin Young Readers Group, 2005

10 9 8 7 6 5 4 3 2 1

THE LIBRARY OF CONGRESS HAS CATALOGED THE DUTTON EDITION AS FOLLOWS:
Silverman, Erica.
When the chickens went on strike / by Erica Silverman: adapted from a story by Sholom Aleichem;
illustrations by Matthew Trueman—1st ed.
p. cm.
Summary: A Jewish boy living in Russia learns a lesson from the village chickens at the time of Rosh ha-Shanah,
the Jewish New Year.
ISBN: 0-525-46862-5 (hc)
1. Jews—Russia—Juvenile fiction. [1. Jews--Russia--Fiction. 2. Rosh ha-Shanah--Fiction.
3. Chickens—Fiction. 4. Behavior--Fiction. 5. Humorous Stories.]
I. Sholom Aleichem, 1859–1916
II. Trueman, Matthew, ill.
III. Title.
PZ7.S58625 Ch 2000 [fic]—dc21 2001040397

Puffin Books ISBN 0-14-240279-6

Manufactured in China

AUTHOR'S NOTE

People all over the world have their own New Year's customs for chasing away bad luck and attracting good, for leaving bad behaviors behind and starting fresh. Kapores is one of these.

The Jewish New Year begins on Rosh Hashanah and ends ten days later on Yom Kippur, the holiest day on the Jewish calendar.

My grandparents made Kapores when my mother was a girl. They held a clucking chicken above my mother's head and said a prayer. My parents did not make Kapores for me, although it was not because the chickens went on strike.

ABOUT SHOLOM ALEICHEM

Sholom Aleichem is the pen name of Sholem Rabinowitz (1859–1916), the great Yiddish author best known for his tales of Tevye the Milkman, which are the basis of the internationally acclaimed play *Fiddler on the Roof.* His chosen name, Sholom Aleichem, is a Yiddish greeting that means "peace be with you."

When the Chickens Went on Strike is adapted from his story "Kapores." A translation by Benjamin Efron appears in *Yiddish Stories for Young People,* edited by Itche Goldberg, published by Kinderbuch Publishers. I wish to thank Mr. Efron, Mr. Goldberg, Ms. Bel Kaufman (author and granddaughter of Sholom Aleichem), and the Sholom Aleichem estate.

Most of all, I am grateful to Sholem Rabinowitz, whose work enlightens and entertains while preserving a portrait of life as it once was in the Jewish communities of Eastern Europe.

Customs come and customs go. I learned this from chickens.

Many years ago in the Russian-Jewish village of my birth, the chickens went on strike. It was Rosh Hashanah, the Jewish New Year. Packed like herring inside the old prayer house, we prayed and promised to be better in the coming year.

More than anything, I longed to be good. I longed to make Papa proud. But when my sister waved from the women's section, I wanted to make her laugh, so I stuck out my tongue.

"Behave!" said Papa.

I tried. But my legs started to swing back and forth, accidentally kicking Beryl the Bigwig.

"Be still!" Papa scolded.

I tried. But then a cool breeze tickled my neck. I craned toward the window, which caused me to topple backward, which caused me to hit the floor. THUD!

"Enough!" hissed Papa. "Go! Wait in the courtyard."

I slunk away, my cheeks burning with shame.

Fresh air! Sunlight! Outside, my spirit soared.

Suddenly I heard a ruckus of clucking and crowing. What was it?
I followed my ears.

Such a sight! Hens, roosters, croakers, chicks!

It was a parade of poultry. A flapping, fluttering frenzy of fowl was fleeing the village.

I followed them over the bridge, along the riverbank, past the mill to a big meadow.

Heart pounding, I hid in tall grass and watched.

A rooster hopped onto a log. *Koo-koo-ree-koo!*, he called out. "Fellow fowl! You know why we are here!"

"Freedom for fowl!" they clucked.

"Rights for roosters!" they crowed.

"Strike! Strike!" they squawked.

The speaker flapped for attention. "Every year at this time, the villagers use us for a strange custom. They grab us and twirl us over their heads. They mumble strange words. They think this will take away their bad deeds."

"The dumb clucks!" heckled a speckled hen.

The rooster went on, "They call this custom Kapores!"

"An end to Kapores!" a spring chicken shrieked.

"No more Kapores!" they all chanted.

No more Kapores? I thought. *I needed Kapores! How else would I get rid of my bad deeds? How would I ever make Papa proud?*

Papa! I raced back. I arrived just as the villagers came pouring out of the prayer house.

"Look at you!" Mama scolded. "Your holiday clothes are filthy."

"The chickens…" I stammered.

Papa took my chin gently in his hand. "These are the holiest days of our year," he said, lifting my face so that I couldn't escape his gaze.

The disappointment in my papa's eyes hurt worse than all of his scoldings put together. I blinked back tears.

"You will stay in the house," Papa said quietly, "and concentrate on how you can be better."

I really tried. But thinking about how to be better made me think about Kapores, which made me think about chickens.

Meanwhile, busy with holiday prayers and preparations, the villagers failed to notice that the chickens were missing ... until it was time for Kapores. Then the women went to the chicken coops. Cries of alarm rang through the village.

"Our chickens are gone!" Mama called out.

"I haven't a hen!" cried the tanner.
"Who took my roosters?" wailed the apple vendor.
"Find my fowl!" shouted the feather plucker.
Everyone searched frantically. They turned the village inside out and upside down.

The women wrung their hands. The men tugged at their beards.

"Did you ever?" said the baker.

"No, never," said the boot maker.

The rabbi's wife gasped, "What will we do for Kapores?"

"Oy! What a catastrophe!"

Everyone chattered at once.

"Don't worry!" I announced. "I know where the chickens are."

They fell silent. They stared down at me.

"Listen," I whispered.

Koo-koo-ree-koo! Kree-kree! Kraw-kraw!

The rabbi's eyes opened wide. "Chickens?" he whispered.

"Chickens," I whispered back.

"Let's go, men!" he said. "Let's get them!"

"Not so fast," said the rabbi's wife. "We women know best how to deal with poultry."

"*Nu?* What are you waiting for?" said the rabbi. "Bring back those birds!"

Armed with sacks of grain, the women set off, proud and determined.

I followed, careful not to be seen.

"*Tsip-tsip. Tsip-tsip,*" the women coaxed, scattering grain.

The fowl scrambled to eat.

"Come, chickens, come. Come home for Kapores." The women crept closer. And closer. They opened their sacks.

Kraw! Kraw! The chickens flew at them, flapping and squawking. "Help!" The women fled frantically back to the safety of the village.

The men laughed. "Afraid of chickens? We will show you how it
is done!"

Armed with sticks, the men marched off.

I followed, certain that now Kapores would be saved.

The men charged. "*Shoo! Shoo!*" They prodded. "Go home, chickens.
It's time for Kapores."

Kraaaaw! Chickens, hens, and roosters sprang as one, tearing at coats, plucking at beards. Feathers filled the air.

Tattered and defeated, the men dragged themselves home.

"Such heroes!" the women scoffed. "You really scared those chickens!"

Too worried to argue, everyone grew silent.

The seamstress sighed. "What do they think they're doing, anyway?"

"They are on strike," I said.

Everyone smirked. Except the rabbi. "Then we must negotiate," he said. "Reb Fishel and I shall speak for the village."

The rabbi's wife raised an eyebrow.

"Also my wife," said the rabbi.

The grain merchant shook a fist. "And when talking fails, we will attack. This time, we will be better prepared."

Shuddering, I followed the team of negotiators.

Chickens, please, I thought, *listen to reason.*

The rabbi approached the crowd. "Worthy fowl, why are you on strike?"

"We demand our rights," said the rooster.

"Rights?" Reb Fishel sneered. "You are chickens!"

There was an angry flutter of wings. "We refuse to be your Kapores!" a chicken shouted.

"*Sha*, good chickens, *sha!*" The rabbi's wife held up her hands. "What if we compromise? We can hold you more gently. We can pray more quickly."

"You can use a turnip!" said the rooster.

"But, chickens," pleaded the rabbi, "we need you for Kapores."

"Is that so?" A broody hen stepped forward. "Where is it written?"

Good question, I thought. *Where is it written?*

"What does it matter to you?" replied the rabbi's wife. "It is a custom of ours from years and years ago."

"An end to your custom!" the chickens chanted.

Reb Fishel wagged a finger at them. "This is a revolution. You chickens want to turn the whole world upside down!"

"We just want our rights!" a chicken cried out. The flock stirred restlessly.

I stepped forward. I could see the horror on the rabbi's face as I crouched among the chickens.

"I have more bad deeds than a dog has fleas," I told them. "Without Kapores, I will never be able to make my papa proud."

The broody hen stared me straight in the eye. "Boychick," she said, "for this, do you really need a chicken?"

Did I? Suddenly I wasn't sure. I was mulling it over when I heard voices from far off. Soon the villagers would attack.

I leaned in close. "I will manage somehow," I whispered. "But you
are in danger! You must leave now!"

The rooster puffed out his chest and flapped his wings. "All freedom-
loving fowl," he commanded, "follow me!"

With that, they turned tail, every last one of them, and strutted off
to parts unknown.

"Chickens, come back!" cried the rabbi's wife.

"We're doomed!" warned the rabbi.

"A plague will befall us," the hay merchant predicted.

Despite many dire predictions, life went on as it always had.

Except that—to everyone's surprise—I managed to be better. Not that I turned into an angel, mind you. I just stopped to think sometimes before I jumped feetfirst into mischief. I was no longer scolded every day. Once I even caught Papa looking at me, his eyes shining with pride.

So you see, customs come and customs go. All things change with time. I learned this from chickens.